Dear Parent:
Your child's love of reading starts here!

Every child learns to read in a different way and at his or her own speed. Some go back and forth between reading levels and read favorite books again and again. Others read through each level in order. You can help your young reader improve and become more confident by encouraging his or her own interests and abilities. From books your child reads with you to the first books he or she reads alone, there are I Can Read Books for every stage of reading:

SHARED READING
Basic language, word repetition, and whimsical illustrations, ideal for sharing with your emergent reader

BEGINNING READING
Short sentences, familiar words, and simple concepts for children eager to read on their own

READING WITH HELP
Engaging stories, longer sentences, and language play for developing readers

READING ALONE
Complex plots, challenging vocabulary, and high-interest topics for the independent reader

ADVANCED READING
Short paragraphs, chapters, and exciting themes for the perfect bridge to chapter books

I Can Read Books have introduced children to the joy of reading since 1957. Featuring award-winning authors and illustrators and a fabulous cast of beloved characters, I Can Read Books set the standard for beginning readers.

A lifetime of discovery begins with the magical words "I Can Read!"

Visit www.icanread.com for information
on enriching your child's reading experience.

Rio 2: Vacation in the Wild

RIO 2 © 2014 Twentieth Century Fox Film Corporation. All Rights Reserved.
Printed in the United States of America. No part of this book may be used or reproduced in any manner whatsoever without written permission except in the case of brief quotations embodied in critical articles and reviews. For information address HarperCollins Children's Books, a division of HarperCollins Publishers, 10 East 53rd Street, New York, NY 10022.
www.icanread.com

ISBN 978-0-06-228499-0

Book design by Victor Joseph Ochoa

13 14 15 16 17   LP/WOR   10 9 8 7 6 5 4 3 2 1   ❖   First Edition

I Can Read!

READING 2 WITH HELP

Blue Sky STUDIOS

Rio 2

VACATION IN THE Wild

by Catherine Hapka

HARPER

An Imprint of HarperCollinsPublishers

It is New Year's Eve in Rio.
The whole city is celebrating!
Blu is having a great time
dancing with his wife, Jewel.

Suddenly, Blu spots his kids.

They are playing near the fireworks.

"We're the last blue Spix's Macaws

on the planet," Blu scolds them.

"We have to stay safe!"

The next morning, Blu makes pancakes
in Linda and Tulio's kitchen.
"Blu, we talked about this,"
Jewel says, sounding annoyed.

Blu doesn't understand
why she is upset.

Linda and Tulio are in the Amazon
on an expedition.

They don't mind if the macaws
use their house.

"What have you got there?"

Blu asks Jewel.

"Breakfast," she says.

She shows him the Brazil nut

she found in the jungle.

She wants the kids to act

like birds instead of people.

Just then the kids call out.

Tulio is on TV!

He is holding up a blue feather
and looking excited.

He and Linda had spotted
a blue Spix's Macaw in the Amazon!
"There may be a whole secret flock
out there," he tells the interviewer.

Jewel is stunned and excited.

"We're not the only ones!" she says.

"There are more of us out there!"

Jewel decides that the whole family
should fly to the Amazon
to find out more.
Blu is nervous, but he agrees.

It is almost time to leave.

Blu checks his fanny pack.

"The GPS!" he exclaims.

He rushes back inside.

Soon he returns with the GPS.

"I programmed in

Linda and Tulio's coordinates,"

he explains.

It is a long flight to the Amazon.

Blu is exhausted

when they reach the river.

The whole family hitches a ride
on a passing boat.
"Good-bye, stinky city air!"
Jewel cries.

Jewel can't wait
to get back to the wild.
But Blu has never lived
in the jungle.

He hopes they can all go back
to the city very soon!

The next day the family

flies away from the boat.

They are deep in the jungle.

Blu pulls out the GPS.

"You have arrived

at your destination," it says.

"See?" Blu says.

"It worked like a charm!"

But there is no sign
of Linda and Tulio.
Blu checks the GPS again.

When he looks up,
his family is gone!
"Where'd everybody go?"
he calls out.
"Jewel? Kids?"

Suddenly talons grab Blu.

He screams in surprise

as an unseen bird carries him away!

"You can't do this to me!"

Blu cries.

"I know my rights!"

The talons let go.

Blu lands on a tree branch.

His family is there.

They are surrounded

by dozens of blue birds

that look just like them!

"We found them!" Jewel cries.

But that isn't all.

The flock's leader appears.

His name is Eduardo,

and he is Jewel's father!

"My little girl," he exclaims.

"All grown up!"

Jewel is thrilled to be

reunited with her family.

Blu is amazed.

This is definitely

the wildest family vacation ever!